Little Platypus

by Nette Hilton
illustrated by Nina Rycroft

Koala Books

Beside the river
in two warm secret places,
one high, one low,
lay two eggs.
Hatching.

Bit by bit, piece by piece,
the shells tipped and tottered . . .
and shifted and shattered.
As eggs do.

First one egg . . .
'A kookaburra!'
the fine mess of feathers said.
'Look at me! I'm a kookaburra!'

Then the other . . .
'Look at me!' the sleek gloss of fur said.
'Look at me! I'm a kookaburra too!'

The pieces of shell were there, bit by tiny bit.
The beak was there, round and flat and soft.

But that was all.
No feathers.
No wings.
Only a sleek glossy fur coat.
Two button-bright eyes and
a tail that wasn't a bird tail at all.

'I'm a kookaburra!'
the small glossy creature declared.

'I don't think so!' laughed the fine mess of feathers.
And with a wonderful swoop of his wonderful wings
the kookaburra flew high into the air.
'Can you do that?' he sang. 'Can you?'

The kookaburra laughed.
As kookaburras do.

The small glossy creature flapped his arms
as hard as a small glossy creature could,
which was not nearly hard enough to fly.

'I don't think I can be a kookaburra,' he said sadly.

And it probably shouldn't have mattered.
Not everyone can be a kookaburra.
But it would have helped, just a little.

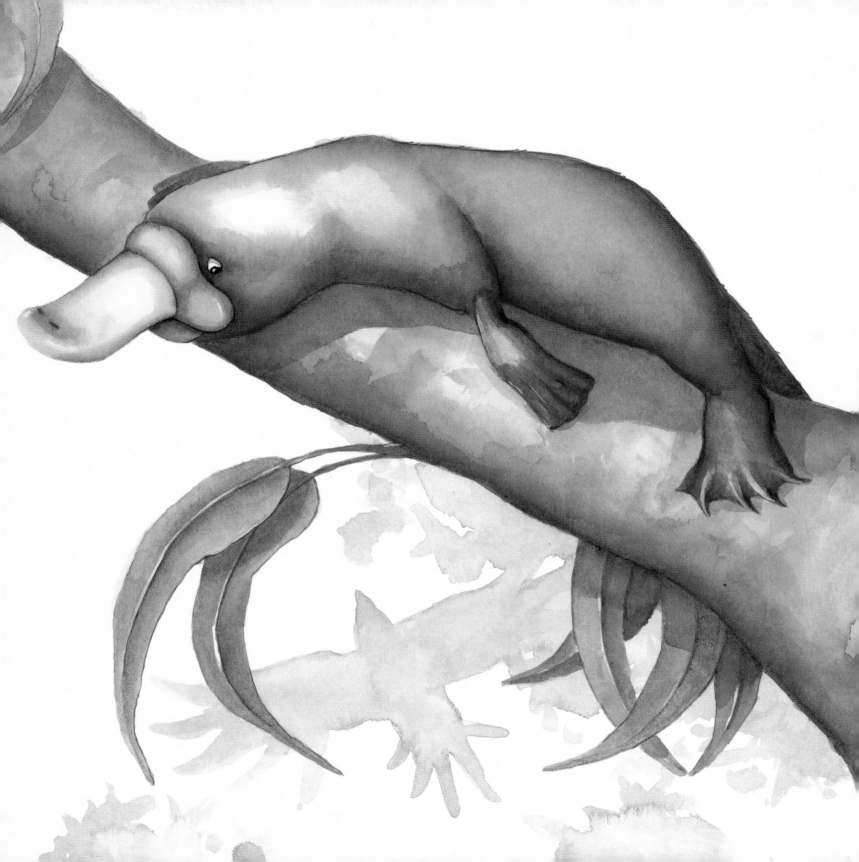

'Who are you?' asked the small glossy creature.
'Am I one of yours?'

'I'm a koala,' said a deep furry voice.
'I climb trees and sit on branches
high above the ground.'

And then, with a soft padded thump
she sat on her soft padded rump,
just as snug as snug could be.
Right up against the fork
of the eucalypt tree.
As koalas do.

The small glossy creature stared at the koala.

The fur was there.
The button-bright eyes were there.
But that was all.
No large ears full of fussy fur.
No round, flat, soft nose.
Only glossy fur, sleek and smooth
and a tail that wasn't a sitting-upon shape at all.

'I don't think I can be a koala,' he said sadly.

And it probably shouldn't have mattered.
Not everyone can be a koala.
But it would have helped, just a little.

'Who are you?' asked the small glossy creature.
'Am I one of yours?'

'I don't think so,' said the tall bird
with a drum in his throat. 'I'm an emu!
I'm tall and elegant and important
and I run very fast indeed.'

And to prove it the emu fluffed his feathers
and pounded off.
As emus do.

'I don't think so either. I'm not an emu!'
the small glossy creature said sadly.

And it probably shouldn't have mattered.
Not everyone can be an emu.
But it would have helped, just a little.

'Who are you?' asked
the small glossy creature.
'Am I one of yours?'

'I'm a wombat!' the sturdy animal
with the sock-top ears spoke.
'Holes is where I live
and digging's what I do best.'

And to prove it she dug deeply
and truly and very, very seriously.
As wombats do.

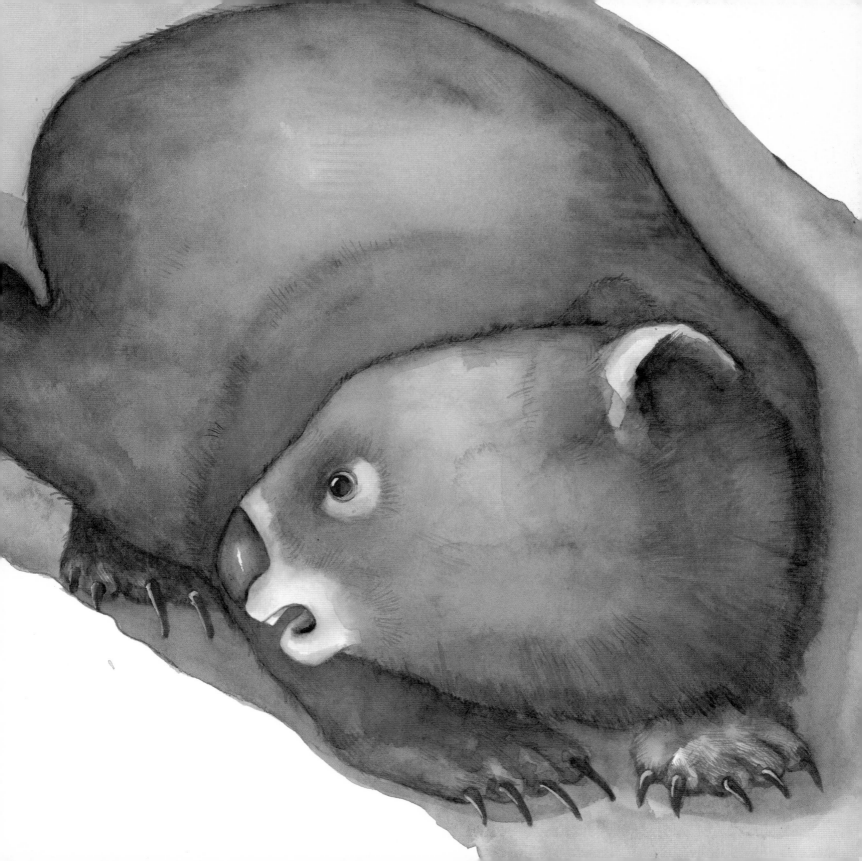

The small glossy creature sighed.
'I don't think I can be a wombat,' he said sadly.

And it probably shouldn't have mattered.
Not everyone can be a wombat.
But it would have helped, just a little.

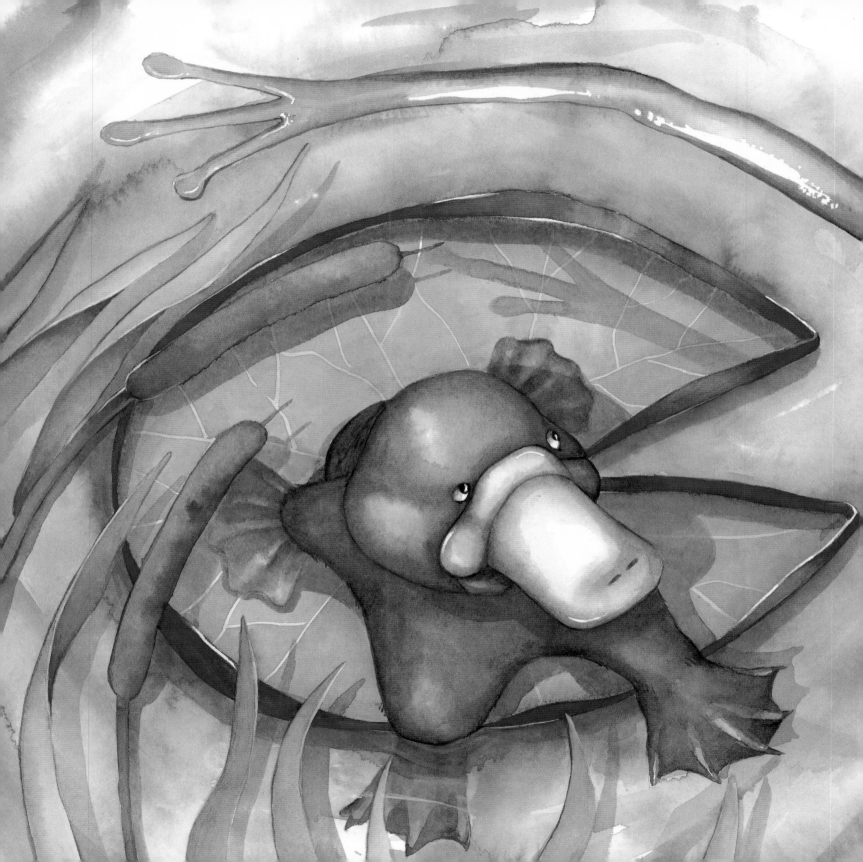

'Who are you?' asked
the small glossy creature.
'Am I one of yours?'

'I'm a frog,' said
the slippery splash of green.
'I come from an egg.
Just like you.'

And the frog leapt into the air.
As frogs do.

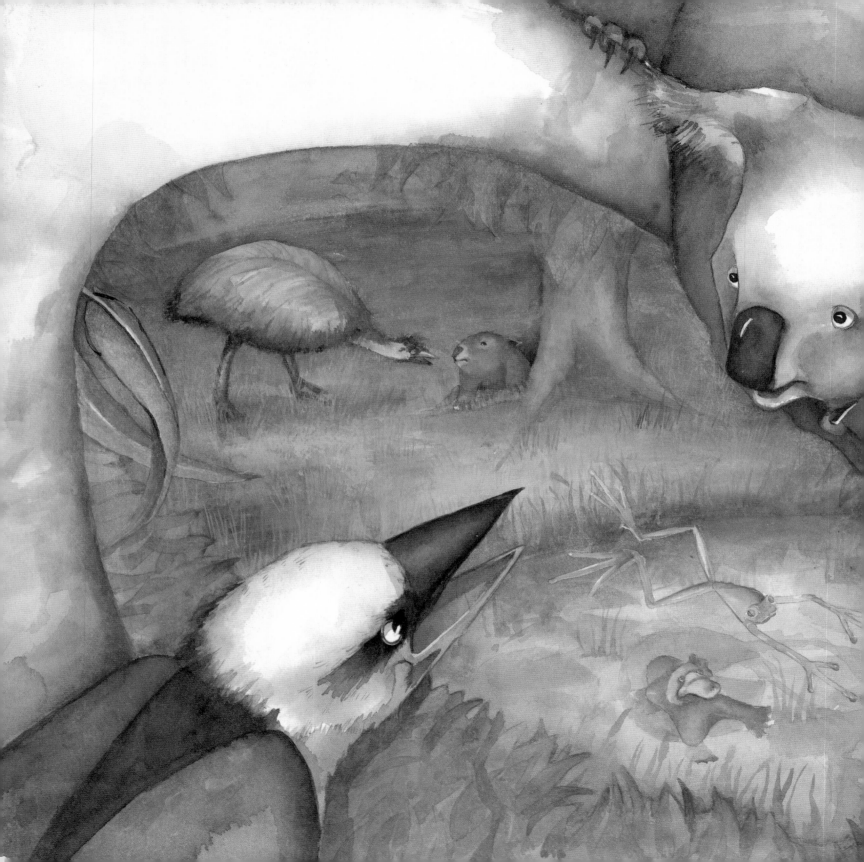

'I don't think I can be a frog,'
the small glossy creature said sadly.

And it probably shouldn't have mattered.
Not everyone can be a kookaburra,
or a koala,
or an emu,
or a wombat,
or a slippery, splashy frog.
But it would have helped ...
Quite a lot, as a matter of fact.

Very large tears rolled down his cheek
and off the end of his soft round nose
and landed, *splot,* in the water.
As tears do.

'Why are you crying?' asked a sleek glossy creature
who popped out of the creek.

'I'm all alone. I don't belong to anyone,'
answered the small glossy creature.
'Am I one of yours?'

Two button-bright eyes. Sleek glossy fur.
A tail that wasn't a bird tail
or a sitting-upon shape.
Webbed bird feet.
And best of all, oh best of all,
a nose round and flat and soft as could be.

'Yes, you are,' said the sleek glossy creature.
'You belong with me.'

'Really?' said the small glossy creature.

'Really,' she said.
'You're a platypus,
just like me!'

And it probably shouldn't have mattered.
But it did!
A whole, great big lot.

And they danced off
into the water.
As platypuses do.

To Nina — with thanks — N.H.
To Andy — thank you so much for always believing in me — N.R.

KOALA BOOKS
First published in Australia in 2000
by Koala Books
4 Merchant St Mascot Australia 2020

Text copyright © Nette Hilton 2000
Illustrations copyright © Nina Rycroft 2000

National Library of Australia CiP data:
Hilton, Nette, 1946- .
Little Platypus.
ISBN 0 86461 272 9.
1. Picture books for children. 1. Rycroft, Nina.
II. Title
A823.3

Produced by Phoenix Offset, printed in China.
9 8 7 6 5 4 3 2 1
05 04 03 02 01 00